李昌憲 著
Poems by Lee Chang-hsien

非馬、許達然、戴珍妮 譯
Translated by William Marr ,Wen-hsiung Hsu,
Jane Deasy

愛河

Love River

李昌憲漢英雙語詩集
Chinese - English

台灣詩叢・Taiwan Poetry Series 05

【總序】詩推台灣意象

叢書策劃／李魁賢

進入21世紀，台灣詩人更積極走向國際，個人竭盡所能，在詩人朋友熱烈參與支持下，策畫出席過印度、蒙古、古巴、智利、緬甸、孟加拉、馬其頓等國舉辦的國際詩歌節，並編輯《台灣心聲》等多種詩選在各國發行，使台灣詩人心聲透過作品傳佈國際間。接續而來的國際詩歌節邀請愈來愈多，已經有應接不暇的趨向。

多年來進行國際詩交流活動最困擾的問題，莫如臨時編輯帶往國外交流的選集，大都應急處理，不但時間緊迫，且選用作品難免會有不週。因此，興起策畫【台灣詩叢】雙語詩系的念頭。若台灣詩人平常就有雙語詩集出版，隨時可以應用，詩作交流與詩人交誼雙管齊下，更具實際成效，對台灣詩的國際交流活動，當更加順利。

以【台灣】為名，著眼點當然有鑑於台灣文學在國際間名目不彰，台灣詩人能夠有機會在國際努力開拓空間，非為個人建立知名度，而是為推展台灣意象的整體事功，期待開創台灣文學的長久景象，才能奠定寶貴的歷史意義，台灣文學終必在世界文壇上佔有地位。

實際經驗也明顯印證，台灣詩人參與國際詩交流活動，很受重視，帶出去的詩選集也深受歡迎，從近年外國詩人和出版社與本人合作編譯台灣詩選，甚至主動翻譯本人詩集在各國文學雜誌或詩刊發表，進而出版外譯詩集的情況，大為增多，即可充分證明。

承蒙秀威資訊科技公司一本支援詩集出版初衷，慨然接受【台灣詩叢】列入編輯計畫，對台灣詩的國際交流，提供推進力量，希望能有更多各種不同外語的雙語詩集出版，形成進軍國際的集結基地。

2017.02.15誌

目次

寄居蟹

日落以後
一隻背著綠貝殼的寄居蟹
苦等月亮
在沙灘上
流
　　　浪
最後仰躺
在碉堡
軀體
虛脫成
一口棺木

1974.12 金門服兵役

聽蘭草訴說

我已感覺不適
華麗的場景
鋼鐵般覆蓋我
　那出售海報使我心悸
　那化學肥料使我衰瘦
　人群的叫價使我暈眩
日光燈
每日逼迫我
為顧客羞怯展示
退逝的容顏

還是放我回山中去
隱居黑黑松林
靜聆淙淙山泉
松子落的時分
目迎歸鳥
目送夕景

共譜一曲純真的音籟
共織一幅唯美的風景

我只是一株蘭草
向自然風雨挑戰
才是我生存的願望

1976.2 谷關

未婚媽媽

1

一支機車鑰匙
神祕的開啟
我緊緊咬住的矜持
在喧嘩中揚長而去
馳風掣電左彎右轉緊急剎車
我本能的緊緊抱住
驚嚇的心浮沉
自己已是獵物

2

起先只是說
一起去烤肉
結果把乾涸的心

烤出春水
微波盪漾

他的每一句話
用力投擲一次又一次
擊中我的十七歲
夢幻般痴醉

羞赧地想偷偷再望他
眸光相遇的觸及
意識底層激盪的情絲
轟然巨響
受父母禁錮的心
湧動未曾有的溫意
感受未曾有的滋味
我把他祕密藏在心底

無論上班或下班，醒或睡
每個時刻以萬縷繫住

美麗的星期天
我如何用心吸住
他丟出的機車鑰匙

3

我不拒絕也不猶疑
跟他進入密樹林裡
他咬一口青蘋果，塞入我嘴內
風兒輕輕的吹
我心亂了也不知
何時撞入他懷裡
唇湄的小船
如魚得水欲潛欲躍

時而萬馬千軍
時而細水潺潺
佔據我真空的世界

他的手忽緩忽急
我的心忽冷忽熱
細胞飽滿碎散
恍惚間，他縛住我
扭動與掙扎的下午
我是被掘開的
河床，浮腫的僵在暴風雨裡
哭泣

4

我的瞳孔放大放大
膽怯望尋揚長而去的機車

輾過柏油路面
再也攤不開夢的碎片
自私的他留給我的是羞憤
孤單忍受刮骨寒風

悽悽弦斷的悲歌
整個街道冷冷清清
一樣的時間一樣是老地方
泣血的心，徘徊張望
街道冷冷清清依然
街燈下，我是唯一的
空心行屍
留下的地址是
一封被退回的信被退回的希望
記憶都生蛆都穿過心臟都
張貼在臉上

5

躲開人潮的囂嚷
躲不開詭異的目光
怯怯進入婦產科醫院
坐立不安的等待
醫生驗血尿，死盯我
突然摘下口罩
冷冷一句
懷孕

能不能打掉
「已有四個月，有生命危險！」
不！我要打掉！
我要——　我——

6

壓抑不住膨脹的恐懼
未辭掉工作就悄悄走了
留下輸送帶旁的空位
日日瞪眼這世界
戲看道德與良知衝擊

1980.4.25

企業無情

驟然宣布
公司營運不善
裁員三分之一

我們聚在一起
焦慮的猜
未公佈的名單

轉眼又屆年終獎金
一年辛苦白枉費
回顧茫茫
手中握著的是西北風
心涼而冷

我們始終是小小的女工
只知道青春被用來燃燒

愈燒
愈短

1980.6

期待曲

每當卡鐘鳴響
挺著圓圓的腹
不堪負荷的加快腳步
趕緊坐在輸送帶旁
繼續投身於生產
用敏捷的手彈唱
愈漲愈高的食衣住行
煩惱波濤似地湧至
被生活包圍起來的汗珠
還能說些什麼
說些什麼呢？

蒼白的臉上精密浮雕
永遠堅強的意志
不僅要度過每一天
度向未來的所有期待
像世世代代勤勞的台灣婦女

自工作中辛苦孕育新的生命
眼中閃亮溫暖的情懷
溶入盛滿的愛
不管汗水掘深額頭幾層

1980.10

臨時工

公司接不到訂單
最先被解僱
走出廠房
我們這些臨時工
臉，掉在路上
被生活踢來踢去

微顫顫地重拾
剩下的自尊，準備隨時拍賣
人口爆炸的加工區
偏逢經濟不景氣
找遍大大小小的公司
再也不能成為依靠

我們嗷嗷待哺
找工作以安定生活
任無情的一紙契約

隨時僱用，也隨時
被解僱

1981.3

勞動之歌

1

快快起來
以自由意志
把上班的路叫醒
跟隨擁擠的人潮前進

為了趕在八點以前
各就工作崗位
頻頻看手錶
調整趕路的步伐

朋友！請不要猛按喇叭
朝陽下的臉都一樣焦急

2

奔流的汗珠
在臉上風乾成鹽
為何灼灼閃亮
記住！只要不心存自卑
揮動辛勤的雙手
我們也能
化渺小為偉大
化短暫為永恆

用盡一生來登臨
繼續成長的梯階

3

我們以恆定的方向
再突破當前的環境
開拓更高深的科技領域
迎接資訊時代

我們是卑微的勞工
在時間與空間的座標上
一步步皆成音符

讓我們把勞心勞力的成果
譜成一首血與汗交響的
勞動之歌

1984.5.1

寶特瓶島

保護生態環境自然景觀
歐美先進國禁止使用

寶特瓶迢遙千里渡重洋
登陸曾經美麗的寶島
從此大部分飲料
特大號免退瓶

多麼不可抗拒
短視近利的商人
盲目愛用的我們

寶特瓶真是摔不破
始終保持豐滿的胴體
愈來愈多的寶特瓶
佔據愈來愈窄的生存空間

島上有限的土地都哭泣
被我們過度糟蹋

美麗的寶島永不再現
難道要留給下一代
觸目驚心的寶特瓶島
在子孫的胸口舐血

1986.9.15

巨變的海與大地

數億年前的海與大地
孕育生命最原始
生物進化的曙光

數千萬年前的海與大地
孕育繁衍動植物
哺乳動物橫行

數萬年前的海與大地
原始人類出現
開始有了掠奪行為

千百年來的海與大地
成為人類爭奪的戰場
被互相殘殺的血染污

十九世紀的海與大地
開始有工業化的污染物滲流
物種面臨生存的威脅

二十世紀的海與大地
無法抗拒嚴重的公害
病變與絕種不斷警告人類

海與大地的未來
將被破壞得生機盡失
人類與所依存的生態系滅絕

1986.10.1

戀的反撲

——工廠裡的故事

陸玉英跟下班亂撞的人潮
擠開往市區的公共汽車
把父母同事的壓力假釋
讓波折凝聚的戀曲
衝出生命的底流

他的歸期是愈來愈近
陸玉英痴迷的想
能再相守——　一夜也好
心情不斷翻湧
恰似夜總會的燈光

陸玉英掩藏不住
萬千情懷總反撲
醉情的她半開半掩
醉酒的他半推半就

他英挺的身影在機場
瘦入陸玉英的胸臆
輾轉打開床頭的燈
夜夜遍尋不來

人都已經回去美國
別再傻下去了
上班給同事逗弄
下班將自己燒痛

1988.5.1

在都市與農村之間

我從農村走向都市

都市
向農村
擴張勢力
土地變了樣
河川改變顏色
我從都市歸回農村
想再接觸自然
原始的面貌
全神聆聽
天地的
呼吸
時隱時顯
寬廣的音域
在靜夜裡流變

再仔細聽，竟是
天與地絕望的控訴

你們人類生生世世是地球上
殘忍的掠奪者濫耕土地砍伐
森林獵殺動物挖掘礦藏製造
廢氣廢水毒害生靈製造武器
興起戰爭肆無忌憚的橫行霸
道切斷生物鏈破壞你們人類
生存的三要素這是盲目的自
殺行為這是盲目的自殺行為

天與地絕望的控訴
從八方圍過來
聲浪愈來愈大
我拔足狂奔

從農村到都市
從都市回農村
在都市與農村之間
頭腦的分析力
開始軟弱無能
被現實趕來趕去

1988.4.15

白髮

早餐的時候
妻吃驚地
你有白髮
開始
拾穗般
邊找邊數

我被生活壓力
壓了又壓，壓了又壓
卻隱藏在黑髮中的白髮
終於被放在我手中

都四十支囉！妻說
我笑了笑
是感覺
有些重量

走下樓梯　準備上班去
秋風吹來涼意
昨日還未被妻發現
我手中的白髮
旋成四十朵白花
掉在孩子成長的路上

1992.5.17

皺紋

晨起洗臉
審視自己的皺紋
被忙碌的生活步調
切開，一條條
皺紋是
溫柔的負擔

1996.4.14

被巨大的水泥高樓包圍

被巨大的水泥高樓包圍
不要怨嘆
缺少綠意的空間

變與不變
看心靈以何種形式
自由自在進出

大都會的小角落
都市生活就在當下
拋開一切
讓紛亂的心靈
停止輸入與輸出

變與不變
看心靈以何種形式
吸取成長的養分

1996.12

生命中的第一場雪

我們同時迎接
生命中的第一場雪
全部亮在雪夜

充滿溫意的燈
照亮過去的心
照亮現在的心
照亮未來的心

心靈與自然的對話
在細雪飄下的午夜
開始

1998.3.1 日本山中湖

我浮在山泉流聲裡

讓山風進來相擁
讓群樹穿窗而入
我浮在山泉流聲裡
身軀很輕很輕
詩境抱著夢境
真是難得的午寐

上班積聚的壓力
被清新的風吹散
被林中的鳥帶走
胸臆很寬很廣
可以容納青翠山巒
有山泉身上流過

傾聽大自然的音籟
充滿想像空間
悠悠醒轉

自己頓成煙嵐一卷
短暫一生
掛在山泉流聲裡

1998.10

綠島監獄

初次踏上綠島
騎機車翻閱索引
血脈賁張的道路

綠島監獄
解嚴後的禁區
只能遠遠地看
緩慢通過，不敢停留

太平洋的季節風
失聲吼叫
生命被踐踏，在這綠島
用血寫在土地上

遊客的耳際，聽見
一群受難者的靈魂
尋找靈魂的出口

1999.3.14 綠島

台灣媽祖

媽祖帶領先民出海
過黑水溝
到台灣數百年
是認同台灣這塊島嶼

台灣媽祖
胸前掛信眾敬獻的
金牌被香火燻得烏金
信仰的歷史
早就落地生根在民間

台灣各地的媽祖
「慈航普渡」
匾額都一樣高高懸掛
保佑斯土斯民

要求赴媚洲進香
要求宗教直航
媽祖什麼也沒說
是有人假借神威吧！

2000.10

黑面琵鷺

站在賞鳥平台
藉高倍數單筒望遠鏡
觀看　黑面琵鷺
成群　站在曾文溪口

相
望

抬頭看著我們人類
黑面琵鷺豎起冠羽
是有所警戒吧
不是歡迎我們

2001.12.23

關廠

用一生的青春歲月
為生活打拚，直到
工廠關閉
才醒覺，中年以後
要面對失業

流著老淚的勞工
有話，嘴唇咬住
無語
而心的傷口
還不斷擴大

走在熟悉的路
相視，無語
雙腳漸感沉重
想回家
無力

2002.2.23

詩，是開啟永恆的鑰匙

蒙古詩人們向我們
握手道別　依依離情
烏蘭巴托的燈火已點亮
兩國詩人們心中的燈火也點亮

我們搭車往烏蘭巴托機場
天空的藍已經看不見了
黑暗遮沒草原
知道我們即將離開

讓我們看一次就難忘
日落草原以後
動人的金黃色絲帶
就懸掛地平線兩頭
這映照久久不散

友誼的手緊緊互握
連結兩國詩人們
在心動深處，握筆寫
詩，是開啟永恆的鑰匙

2005.7

南亞海嘯

地殼鬱積的能量
自海底瞬間暴裂
澎湃洶湧的巨浪
毀滅性的襲擊

人類的生命被吞噬
捲入海中漂流
陸地橫屍遍野
人間的悲慘視界

海嘯過後滿目瘡痍
悽慘恐怖的影像傳播
震驚全世界的心
留下那個舉目無親的小孩

站在災難現場
眼淚都已經哭乾了

還舉頭望向天空
無助的哭喊

2005.12.25

春雨

半夢半醒半睡
妳的手習慣
跨越我的土地

感覺暖流
相遇
乾渴的土地

好久不見
春雨
來得正是時候

2007.10

回鄉偶詩

爸爸問我：多久沒回家了
掛鐘在牆上側臉竊笑
又要說工作忙碌
時間被切割得零碎

我反問自己：多久沒抬頭看星星了
在二十四小時生產的電子工廠
經理真不是人幹的，隨時待命
出差在蘇州在上海在台北在竹科
早已把星光遺忘

可是我離家多遠多久
心裡真的想要回家
回到出生地南化區
回到無光害的山居
紅瓦老屋的庭院
仍留有我觀星的夢

能夠辦理退休
證明我不再年輕
頭髮兩鬢早已灰白
想：星星是否也會老
星星用閃爍代替回答

仰望滿天星星的感動
一整夜我沒有睡
思考人生的奧義
其實只要簡單過生活
親近大自然的美好
讓心靈歸於平靜

2006.2.6 離台返蘇州寫於機上

族譜

回到老家大廳
爸爸戴上老花眼鏡
兩人共同審視
留傳下來的手抄族譜

突然躍出爸爸記憶
他指著久遠的名字
轉述聽說的口傳故事
名字被叫醒　在午夜
感覺有一種悲涼

增補各房今人的名字
重新抄寫在稿紙上
準備印刷分送族人
在這容易失傳的時代

代代名字串起來
族譜　是一條項鍊
掛在後代子孫的脖子上
不因社會變遷　而失去
血脈的張力

2008.2.6

壁虎

倒掛在天花板
壁虎自認是霸主
守在制高點
耐心等候飛蛾

持續撲向日光燈
飛蛾暈頭轉向時
壁虎趁機捕殺
吞下肚腹

永不飽足
慾望之眼圓睜
強勢控制生存空間

壁虎的形體
不斷自我膨脹

直到整個地球
支離破碎

2008.7.5

繫夢

妻的長髮是船纜
繫住我夢的小船
我用力　拚命划

回到家
習慣叫了一聲
妻的小名

夢醒
滿身大汗
窗外蘇州春雪

握著的手
竟是自己
卻回不了家

2006.2.14 蘇州

鐵柵內的母乳牛

母乳牛剛生產
小乳牛剛站起來
母奶還來不及喝
被陌生人強制抱離

關在鐵柵內的母乳牛
沒有可以活動的空間
整天站立往外望
想起小寶貝

小乳牛想念母親
想喝一口母奶
得靠想像力

人類不用母奶哺育
嬰兒長大以後才知道
嬰兒奶粉是牛乳製成

自己的媽媽是母乳牛
被關在鐵柵內

2008.10.11

白鷺鷥

——紀念二二八

孤單的白鷺鷥
縮著一隻腳獨立
面向愛河
一言不發

早凋的英靈
重回現場參加
紀念二二八活動
六十二週年一晃而過

想及歷史性的傷口
再度爆開
鮮血染紅圓山
飯店外棍棒侍候

整個下午白鷺鷥
縮著一隻腳獨立

思索下一步
怎麼飛出去

2009.6

螢火蟲

螢火蟲孤單的飛
來我書房尋找失聯的弟兄
飛得非常疲累了
停在台灣古地圖上

被殖民被外來政權統治
手繪的古老地圖流著淚
長期被予取予求
生命遭受到迫害威脅

我緊張的關掉電燈
怕有線民密報

螢火蟲自顧的發光
企圖照亮台灣地圖
這塊有歷史意義的土地
這塊有固定疆域的島國

2009.6

蘆葦花

趕赴秋天的約會
蘆葦花彎腰梳理
滿頭白髮

承受不景氣的壓力
越梳　越稀
越理　越白

2009.12

露珠

——紀念結婚三十年

剛醒來的陽光
輕柔觸及昨夜
留在花瓣上的露珠

我專注尋找最美好的視角，要
妳成為我心中唯一
閃亮鑽石光芒的露珠

相遇生命中的紅粉知己
必有一段因緣，來自無明
當因緣俱足，才相識
多麼不容易啊

結婚三十年一晃而過
感知人生如此短暫
露珠啊！妳正驚慌
青春美麗即將消失

我用數位影像留住
妳的美麗光芒，在我心中
永不消失，永不消失

我同時將記憶儲存
在雲端，等待
老來相依相伴

2009.12

非人

妻說
我被你的鼾聲
吵醒

驚覺
自己困倦如屍
活著

軀體
被工作切割成
碎片

靈魂
看見人與人互相踐踏
哭泣

2010.10

帶路雞

公雞母雞合關一籠
公雞有逃跑的舉動
母雞有逃走的意思

同時被關入舊行李箱
跟著新娘一起出嫁
從舊部落到大都市

暈車的公雞突然睜眼
看見一絲絲光而興奮
伸長脖子開始叫

喔喔喔喔喔喔喔
行李箱內母雞
緊閉眼睛想像

2011.9

聽令於主人

總會在機場轉機候機
遇見許多相識的
流浪之鴿

來自不同的鴿舍
各擁不同的旗號
卻都聽令於主人

按照主人的指令
一生為主人奔波
流浪在世界各地

按照主人的意志
只能說：是
才能擁有一片
不屬於自己的天空

2011.10

愛河

Love River
我們心中有一條河
用愛與浪漫寫滿

Love River
愛河水慢慢流
向時間深處

Love River
流入血脈成為
內在心靈的力量

Love River
詩意與美感
裝滿人生旅程

2010.11.18.

戰爭與和平紀念公園

紀念二二八
追思台籍老兵
都是苦難的靈魂

政治劊子手血腥射殺
槍聲卡住記憶
恐懼恆常在

獨裁統治者下台
人民的生命財產
可以不再被剝奪嗎

戰爭與和平紀念公園
追思的人散了
英靈不散

看見自己胸口
插上二十一世紀的茉莉花
全世界遍地開

2013.4.15

美麗島站

他說：想躺下來欣賞
光之穹頂玻璃藝術
在民主自由的美麗殿堂
具歷史性意義的美麗島站
讓多樣色彩包容
今生今世經歷的一切

躺下來，他也看不清楚
光之穹頂玻璃藝術
美，成為他的過去式
想起事件那晚他在台下
眼睛飽受催淚瓦斯攻擊
一個小市民如何抵擋
有計畫有組織的鎮壓憲警

許多歷史上的錯誤
許多無辜犧牲的生命

沒有喚醒暗藏的血腥
黑手如果可以及時反省
真正的民主就不會倒退
人們不必互相對立衝突

看得見與看不見的界線
消失。可能嗎？
他說：人啊！死亡才會躺下來
欣賞光之穹頂玻璃藝術
在民主自由的美麗殿堂
具歷史性意義的美麗島站

2013.6

心咖啡

手裡拿著相同的咖啡杯
心裡卻有不同的形狀

同樣品嘗東山單品咖啡
心中各自解讀色香味

生命歷程的樂、喜、怒、哀
透過語言、文字、音符、顏料詮釋

咖啡世界充滿想像
無界無邊任遨遊

啊！沒形狀的咖啡香
讓心靈充分自由

2013.8.30

楓紅

楓紅是季節的容顏
濡染詩意又暗藏感傷

那種美最讓人心靈悸動
揹著相機追去奧萬大
兩年兩次只見落葉滿地

想拾起一些作紀念
情緒陷入楓紅深層
雙腳動彈不得

2013.9

台灣茶山行旅

台灣茶山行旅
茶在心中
人在畫中

走訪製茶達人
品茶香　知日月
精華　盡在一杯茶湯

撲鼻茶香
富韻茶湯
導順五臟六腑
舒暢十二經脈

台灣茶是甘泉
溫潤台灣人的心
豐富台灣人的生活

2013.10

人

人隨緣生滅
人輪迴來去

人的靈魂離開一個軀殼
人的靈魂依附一個軀殼

人離開這世間的家庭
人來到這世間的家庭

人奔波忙碌之後
回到出生時的家
心靜下來研讀
般若波羅密多心經

二六〇個字蘊藏浩瀚的真義
每一個字都是天宇中
發出亮光的星球

靜聽祖厝的簷滴聲聲快
想必露水凝重出清涼音
家　迴盪著這一生

2014.2

詩人作陶

我用寫許多詩的手
隨意捏出許多茶杯
不求平整不求完美
各具形態似圓非圓
相應於真實人生
凡捏過必留下手感

我用寫許多詩的手
在轆轤上拉胚
把人生拉成圓
泥土的可塑性
激發我的創作力持續
探索藝術表現的形式

2014.2

網路

網路，什麼都有
手指滑來滑去
催眠自己
網路沒有距離

按一下讚
加入好友、粉絲群
LINE來、賴去
隨時保持待機

越來越多人的自我
受智慧型手機控制
像染上毒隱
經常性發作

在網路社群中
每個人都在找尋
寂寞的存在

2014.6.15

界限

我的思想
跟隨風
穿越

人類界定的海域
人類界定的國界
人類界定的時間
人類界定的空間

界限
一切都無
盡　消失

2014.9.15

人與海

人類生生世世
用貪婪的心
想要擁有海

海無時無刻
以波浪清洗
人類貪婪的心

2014.9.15

星光

星光滿天
這裡無公害
有人對著星空
進行長時間曝光

留下星軌
漂亮的光跡
如果形成圓
夢中也會笑

無量的星球
運行不已
問誰將與浩瀚宇宙接軌

許多不可思議不可測度的
生命，在遙遠的星球
招手，呼喚地球人

2014.4.27

螢光

國有林地無污染
暗夜裡螢火蟲紛飛
點點螢光冷冷測度

生活在壓力鍋的
現代人，有必要來此
接受螢火蟲加持

閃爍以微弱的冷光
療養現代人心靈深處
無名的那種空虛

有人，對著螢光
進行長時間曝光
留下漂亮的光跡

神祕的抽象畫
天使微醉時
留下的草書

2014.4.27

阿塱壹古道行旅圖

落山風在林間呼嘯
風雨阻擋不了我們
靠豐富的想像與期待
走一趟阿塱壹古道

巨浪一波波拍岸嚇阻
海面吹來強風迎面痛擊
只能側身逆風低頭
循先民的足跡前進

耳邊響起鼕鼕鼓聲
是歷史遠端的回音
至今仍留在此
山崖海岸間跳動

一天捲動數百年歷史
置身如此壯闊的場景

感動來自生命深處
每個人都烙印一幅長卷
阿塱壹古道行旅圖

2015.10.20

作者簡介

李昌憲，台南人，1954年出生，現居高雄市。曾參加「森林詩社」、「綠地詩社」、「陽光小集」、「笠詩社」。曾任職上市電子公司經理，創作以詩文、篆刻、陶藝、攝影為主。現為《笠》詩刊主編，高雄市第一社區大學篆刻老師。

1981年6月出版第一本詩集《加工區詩抄》，並於1982年獲笠詩獎。其他出版詩集《生態集》（1993年）、《生產線上》（1996年）、《仰觀星空》（2005年）、《從青春到白髮》（2005年）、《台灣詩人群像・李昌憲詩集》（2007年）、《台灣詩人選集・李昌憲集》（2010年）、《美的視界——慢遊大高雄詩攝影集》（2014年）、《高雄詩情——1977-2015》（2016年）。詩作〈期待曲〉詩句被選入【高雄市文學步道】；詩作〈加班〉、〈企業無情〉被選入【科大國文選】；及年度詩選、國內外之詩選集，被以英、日、韓、西、蒙等文字翻譯及介紹。

譯者簡介

非馬，出版有23本詩集（其中兩本為英文，其它為中文），3本散文集，以及幾本譯著。他的詩被譯成十多種文字並被收入百多種選集，包括台灣，大陸，英國及德國的高中和大學教科書。他曾擔任過美國伊利諾州詩人協會的會長，並獲得台灣、大陸及美國的詩創作及翻譯獎。現居美國芝加哥地區。

許達然，任教美國西北大學三十五年（1969-2004），退休為榮譽教授。2007年至2011年回台灣擔任東海大學歷史研究所講座教授。東海大學歷史畢業，哈佛大學碩士，芝加哥大學博士，牛津大學Balliol學院英國社會史博士後研究。

戴珍妮，生於愛爾蘭，長於台灣，現居溫哥華的中英文譯者，並為加拿大卑詩省翻譯者學會準會員，以及加拿大文學翻譯者協會（位於蒙特婁康考迪亞大學）會員。

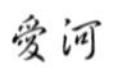

Love River

Love River

Hermit Crab

After the sun sets

A hermit crab carrying a green shell on its back

Painstakingly awaits the moon

W a n

d e r s

On the beach

And finally lies on its back

On a fort

And collapses into

A coffin

December 1974, military service in Kinmen
(Translated by Jane Deasy)

Listen to What the Bluegrass Says

I already feel unwell
Splendid scenes
Cover me like iron and steel
    That for sale poster makes my heart palpitate
    Those chemical fertilizers make me feeble and thin
    The crowd's bidding makes me faint and dizzy
The fluorescent light
Forces me everyday
To shyly display for the customers
My lost and faded looks

Or let me return to the mountains
To live in seclusion in the black pine forest
Silently listening to the swooshing mountain spring
The moment when the pine nut falls
My eyes greet the returning birds
My eyes see off the scene of sunset

Composing together a song of pure sounds
Weaving together a scenery of beauty

I'm only a blade of bluegrass
To challenge nature, wind, and rain
Is the true wish of my existence

February 1976, Guguan
(Translated by Jane Deasy)

Unmarried Mother

1

A moped key
Mysteriously opens
My tightly bitten constraint
Speeding away in the clamour
Swift as the wind, quick as lightening, turning left and right,
slamming on the brakes
I instinctively tightly hold on
My frightened heart heaves
I myself have already become prey

2

At first we had only said
We would go together to have a barbecue

It turned out that our parched hearts
Had spring waters roasted out of them
Rippling waves throughout the water

His every sentence
Forcefully tossed, again and again
And hit my seventeen year old
A dream-like intoxication

I felt ashamed to want to secretly look at him again
The touch of our eyes meeting
The stirring threads of emotion at the bottom layer of my consciousness

Sounded with a tremendous loud bang
My heart that was imprisoned by my parents
Surged with a warmth that was never before
Experienced a taste that was never before

I hid his secrets in the depths of my heart

No matter if I was at work or not, if asleep or awake

In every moment I would bind it with ten thousand threads

A beautiful Sunday

How I diligently sucked on

The moped key that he threw out

3

I did not refuse and did not hesitate to

Go with him into the dense woods

He bit a mouthful of green apple, and stuffed it into my mouth

A breeze gently blew

I was confused and did not know

When I fell into his arms

The little boats on banks of my lips
Desired to dive and to jump like fish in water
At times thousands and thousands of soldiers and horses
At times a tiny stream gently flowing by
Seizing my void world

His hands moved fast one moment and slow at the next
My heart was cold one moment and hot at the next
Cells filled up, fragmented and scattered
In an instant, he tied me down
An afternoon of twisting and struggling
I am an excavated
Riverbed, swollen and rigid in a storm
Crying

4

My pupils dilate and dilate
I timidly gaze at the moped speeding away
Rolling over the asphalt surface
The fragments of my dreams can no longer be unfolded
Selfish him, leaving me with shame and resentment
Enduring the bone-chilling winds in solitude
Sorrowful broken strings in a song of lament
The entire street is desolate
The same time, the same old place
A heart is crying tears of blood, lingering and watching
The deserted roads remain
Under the streetlights, I am the only one
An empty-hearted walking corpse
The address left behind is a returned letter, returned hope

Maggots have already grown on the memories and have passed
through the heart
Plastered on the face

5

Escaping from the clamour of the crowd
Cannot escape the strange looks
Enter timidly into the women's hospital
Restlessly waiting
The doctor tests the blood and urine, giving me a death stare
He suddenly takes off his mask
And coldly says
Pregnant

Can it be taken away
"You're already four months along, it would be life-threatening!"

No! I want it taken away!

I want—I—

6

The expanding fear cannot be suppressed

I quietly leave my job without resigning

An empty space beside the conveyor belt remains

Staring day after day at this world

Playfully watching the collision of morals and conscience

April 25, 1980

(Translated by Jane Deasy)

Ruthless Enterprises

A sudden announcement
The company has been operating poorly
One-third of the employees will be laid off

We gather together
Anxiously guessing
The unannounced list of names

In a flash it is once again time for our year-end bonus
A year of hard work wasted
Looking back, boundless and vast
Holding the northwest wind[1] in one's hands
The heart is bitter and cold

We have always been small worker women
We only know that our youth has been used to burn

The more it burns

The shorter it becomes

Note 1:Northwest wind, to "drink the northwest wind", a Chinese idiom, meaning to be without food or drink due to poverty.

June, 1980
(Translated by Jane Deasy)

Song of Hope

Every time the bell rings, the pregnant woman rushes back to the production line
Her round belly weighing heavily on her feet

Sitting beside the belt conveyor
She continues her task
And sings of the ever-increasing cost of living
While worries come like waves
Splashing onto her forehead then flowing down in beads of perspiration

A delicate relief print emerges
On her pallid face
A strong will to live not only today
But also thousands of days
In the future of hope
She painstakingly nurtures new life with her work

Like generations and generations of industrious Taiwanese women
Warm feeling shines in her eyes
While love flows with sweat
In the deep groves on her forehead

October 1980
(Translated by William Marr)

Temporary Workers

Business is slack at the company
We, the temporary workers
Are the first ones to go
Our faces, have fallen to the ground
And are kicked around by life

Tremblingly we pick up the pieces of our self-respect
And wait for another auction
In this depressed zone
But there is no bidder

Clamoring for food
We search for work
Letting a piece of heartless contract
Hire at any time
And fire at any time

March, 1981
(Translated by William Marr)

Song of Labour

1

Quickly get up
With free will
Awaken the road to go to work
Follow the jam-packed crowds and proceed

To rush and be before eight o' clock
Each at one's own post
Looking at one's watch again and again
Adjusting hurried steps

Friend! Please don't honk your horn so fiercely
Faces under the morning sun are all equally anxious

2

The racing beads of sweat

Are dried into salt by the wind

Why does it glisten brightly

Remember! As long as there is no feeling of inferiority in the heart

By waving our industrious hands

We can also

Make the small, great

Make the transient, eternal

To spend a lifetime climbing

A step on the ladder of continuous growth

3

With a constant direction we
Again break through the immediate environment
Develop higher realms of science and technology
To welcome the Information Age

We are humble labourers
On the coordinates of time and space
Each and every step become musical notations

Allow us to use the fruits of the labour of our bodies and minds
To compose a symphony of sweat and blood
A song of labour

May 1, 1984
(Translated by Jane Deasy)

Island of PET Bottles

The protection of ecological environments and natural landscapes
Progressive nations in Europe and the United States have prohibited
the use

PET bottles cross thousands of miles of distant oceans
To land on a once beautiful precious island
From here on most beverages
Their extra large size bottles are exempt from bottle returns

How irresistible
Short-sighted merchants
Us who blindly love to use them

PET bottles truly don't break when they fall
Always maintaining a plump carcass
More and more PET bottles
Occupy the narrowing living space

The scant land on the island all weeps
It has been excessively ravaged

The beautiful precious island is never to be seen again
Is it that we want to leave our next generation
An island of PET bottles that shocks the eye and startles the heart
To lick blood off the chests of our children and grandchildren

September 15, 1986
(Translated by Jane Deasy)

The sea and the earth in Great Transformation

The sea and the earth several hundred-million years ago
Bred the dawn
Of the evolution of the most primitive life.

The sea and the earth millions of years ago
Bred and multiplied animals and plants,
And the mammals wet on the rampage.

The sea and the earth several ten-thousand years ago
Homo sapiens appeared
And began to plunder.

The sea and the earth in the past millennium
Have become the battle field of human struggle
Stained with blood of mutual carnage.

The sea and the earth in the nineteenth century
Began to be industrialized to produce pollution
To threaten the existence of the species.

The sea and the earth in the twentieth century
Were unable to resist grave public disaster.
Diseases and extinction consistently cautioned
Mankind.

The future of the sea and the earth
Would be ruined without any signs of life.
Mankind and the ecological system would be annihilated.

October 1, 1986
(Translated by Wen-hsiung Hsu)

A Counter-Offensive Love

——A story at the factory

Lu Yu-Ying followed the crowd after work
And pressed her way onto a bus heading downtown
She put aside the pressures from her parents and her co-workers
And let the frustrating love song
Rush out of the undercurrent of her life

He will return soon
Lu Yu-Ying thinks in her blind passion
It's nice to be together – even just for one night
Her mind is in a turmoil
Like the lights of the nightclub

Lu Yu-Ying is unable to conceal
The loving mood that is constantly fighting
Back
drunk with love, she is half-open, and half-shut

drunk with liquor, he is half-pushing, and
half-pulling

At the airport his handsome figure
slipped into Lu Yu-Ying's breast
again and again she turned on the bed lamp
yet night after night he never appeared

He is long gone back to America
Don't go on kidding yourself
Don't let co-workers tease you at work
Don't burn yourself after work

May 1, 1988
(Translated by William Marr)

Between the City and the Countryside

I walk from the countryside towards the city

The city
Expands its force
Towards the countryside
The land has changed
The color of rivers have changed
I return from the city to the countryside
And want to make contact again with nature
The primitive appearance
Fully listening to
Heaven and earth's
Breathing
Now hidden, now appearing
A broad range of sound
Flows and changes in the silence of the night

To listen carefully once again, it is in fact
The desperate accusations of heaven and earth

You, mankind, from generation to generation are the ruthless predators of this planet
Over-plowing the land, lumbering forests, hunting and killing animals
Mining minerals, producing wastewater
Poisoning creatures, manufacturing weapons and provoking war
Recklessly tyrannizing
Amputating the biological chain
Destroying the three elements of your human existence
This is a blindly suicidal action
This is a blindly suicidal action

The desperate accusations of heaven and earth
Surround me from all directions

The sound of waves becomes louder and louder
I take to my heels and run like mad

From the countryside to the city
From the city to the countryside
Between the city and the countryside
The mind's analytical power
Begins to become weak and lacking in strength
Hurtled back and forth by reality

April 15, 1988
(Translated by Jane Deasy)

White Hair

During breakfast
Startled, my wife said
You have white hair
And began
Searching and counting
Like gleaning after a harvest

I am pressured and pressured, pressured and pressured
By life's pressures
Yet it's hidden in the white hair among the black hair
It has finally been put into my hands

I've already found 40 hairs! My wife says
I crack a smile
It feels like
There is some weight

Walking down the stairs, getting ready to go to work
The autumn wind blows a slight chill
Yesterday my wife didn't even notice
The white hairs in my hand
Spun into forty white flowers
And fell onto the paths of growth of my children

May 17, 1992
(Translated by Jane Deasy)

Wrinkles

Getting up in the morning, washing my face

Examining my own wrinkles

The busy pace of life

Sliced open, line after line

Wrinkles are

A gentle burden

April 14, 1996

(Translated by Jane Deasy)

Surrounded by Giant Cement Towers

Surrounded by giant cement towers
Don't sigh with resentment
At the spaces lacking greenery

Change and no change
See with which form the soul
Freely comes and goes

Small corners in the metropolis
City life, is in that moment
Everything is set aside
To stop the input and output
Of the chaotic soul

Change and no change
See with which form the soul
Absorbs nutrients to grow

December 1996
（Translated by Jane Deasy）

The First Snow of a Lifetime

At the same time, we welcomed
The first snow of our lifetime
All glowed in the snowy night

The light that is full of warmth
Illuminates my heart from the past
Illuminates my heart at the present
Illuminates my heart in the future

The dialogue between my soul and nature
At midnight with fluttering light snow
Begins

March 1, 1998
Lake Yamanaka, Japan
(Translated by Jane Deasy)

I Float Amongst the Sounds of Mountain Springs

Let the mountain winds in and embrace
Let the trees stretch through the windows and come in
I float amongst the sounds of mountain springs
The body is so light, so light
Poetic imagery holds on to dreamland
What a truly rare sound afternoon sleep

The pressures built-up from work
Are blown away by the fresh winds
Taken away by the birds of the forest
Inner feelings are so vast, so vast
That they can contain the verdant mountains
With mountain springs flowing past my body

Listen to the sounds of nature
Full of room for imagination
I awaken and turn unhurriedly

After a pause I become a roll of smoke and mist

A short life

Suspended in the sounds of mountain springs

October 1998

(Translated by Jane Deasy)

Green Island Prison

The first time I stepped onto Green Island
I rode a moped to read the index
Of its roads' expanding blood vessels

Green Island Prison
A restricted area after martial law ended
It could only be looked at from afar
To slowly pass through, without daring to stop

The seasonal winds of the Pacific Ocean
Screams and cries until its voice is gone
Life has been trampled upon, on this Green Island
Written with blood upon the earth

The ears of the tourists, hear

A group of victims' souls

Search for an exit for the souls

March 14, 1993 Green Island
(Translated by Jane Deasy)

Mazu of Taiwan

Mazu led our ancestors out to sea
Across the black gutterway
Over the several hundred years in Taiwan
She has acknowledged this island of Taiwan

Mazu of Taiwan
On her chest hangs a golden medallion
Offered with reverence by the faithful and blackened by the smoke
of incense
The history of faith
Has long been rooted among the people

The Mazus all over Taiwan
"Ferries of salvation"
Are all the same hanging up high on the inscribed boards
Blessing and protecting this land and this people

Demanding to make a pilgrimage to Meizhou

Demanding that there be direct routes for religious purposes

Mazu has said nothing at all

It must be man that takes advantage of the might of the gods !

October 2000

(Translated by Jane Deasy)

Black-faced Spoonbill

Standing on the bird-watching platform
Through a high-magnification monocular lens
Watching, the black-faced spoonbill
In flocks, standing on the Zengwen estuary

Looking
At one another

Raising their heads to see us humans
The black-faced spoonbill raises their crown feathers
It must be a sense of alertness
And not a welcome for us

December 23, 2001
(Translated by Jane Deasy)

Factory Closure

With life's years of youth
Have strove hard to live, until
The factory closed
It was only then that I became aware, after middle age
I would be facing unemployment

The workers weep bitter tears
They have things to say, their lips are bitten shut
Without words
And the heart's wound
Is continuously expanding, too

Walking along a familiar road
Looking at each other, without words
Our feet feel gradually heavy

I want to go home

No strength

February 23, 2002

(Translated by Jane Deasy)

Poetry, a Key That Unlocks Eternity

The Mongolian poets

Shake our hands and bid farewell, reluctantly parting way

Lights have been lit in Ulaanbaatar

Lights in the hearts of the poets of two countries have been lit too

We journey towards Ulaanbaatar Airport

The blue of the sky can not longer be seen

Darkness cloaks over the grasslands

Knowing that we are about to depart

Allow us one look and we cannot forget

After sunset on the grasslands

The touching golden ribbons

That suspend on both ends of the horizon

The shine reflects and lingers a good while

Hands of friendship tightly grasp each other
Connecting the poets of two countries
In deep feelings , I hold a pen to write
Poetry, a key that unlocks eternity

July 2005
(Translated by Jane Deasy)

South Asian Tsunami

The pent-up energy of the earth's crust
Exploded in an instant from the bottom of the sea
The surging, turbulent giant waves
A devastating raid

Human life was devoured
Dragged into the sea to drift by the current
The land is corpse-strewn
A tragic vision in our mortal world

Scenes of devastation are everywhere after the tsunami
Images of wretched horror are spread
Shocking the heart of the entire world
Leaving behind the little children with no kin to turn to

Standing at the scene of the disaster
Tears have already been cried dry

Still, heads are raised towards the sky
To helplessly cry and shout

December 25, 2005
(Translated by Jane Deasy)

Spring Rain

Half dreaming, half awake, half asleep
Your hands have the habit of
Crossing on to my land

It feels as if a warm current
Has met
A parched, thirsty land

Long time no see
Spring rain
You have come just in time

October 2007
(Translated by Jane Deasy)

A Fortuitous Poem on Returning Home

Dad asks me: How long have you not been home
The hanging clock on the wall turns its face to the side and laughs in
its sleeve
I will have to say again that it's been busy at work
Time has been cut into fragments

I turn and ask myself: How long has it been since I've raised my head
to watch the stars
In an electronics factory with 24-hour production
The managerial job truly isn't meant for humans, on standby at any time
On business trips to Suzhou, to Shanghai, to Taipei, to Hsinchu
Science Park
I have long-forgotten the starlight

But how long and how far have I been away from home
In my heart I truly want to return home

To return to the place of my birth, Nanhua District
To return to my light pollution-free home in the mountains
In the courtyard of the old red-tiled house
My star-watching dreams still remain there

To be able to retire
Proves I am no longer young
The hair on my temples has long been grey
To think: do the stars age too
The stars glisten in reply

How striking it is to raise one's head to a sky full of stars
The entire night, I did not sleep
Reflecting on the profound meaning of life
In fact as long as one can simply live their life

To get close to the beauty of nature

To allow the heart and soul to return to tranquility

February 6, 2006
Written on the plane leaving Taiwan returning to Suzhou
（Translated by Jane Deasy）

Family Tree

Returning to the hall in my old home
Dad is wearing reading glasses
The two of us survey together
The handwritten family tree that was handed down

Suddenly leaping out of Dad's memory
He points to the names from of old
And relays stories he heard through the oral tradition
The names were waken up, at midnight
It feels like there is a sort of desolation

Adding and compiling the names of those there today in each room
Copying them out afresh on manuscript paper
Preparing to print and distribute them to our clanspeople
In this era where things easily fail to be passed down

String together the names from generation to generation

The family tree, is a necklace

That hangs from the necks of our descendants

Social changes will not cause

The bloodline's tension, to be lost

February6, 2008

(Translated by Jane Deasy)

Gecko

Hanging upside down from the ceiling
The gecko reckons himself an overlord
Guarding the high grounds
Patiently waiting for a flying moth

Continuously fluttering towards the fluorescent light
When the moth is dizzily turning
The gecko seizes its chance, it hunts and kills
And swallows into his belly

Never satiated
The staring eye of desire
Mightily controlling living space

The form of the gecko
Continuously self-inflates

Until the whole world

Fragments

July 5, 2008

(Translated by Jane Deasy)

Bound Dreams

My wife's long hair is the boat's tow rope
Bound to my dream's little boat
I exert my strength, I row for my life

When I return home
I am used to calling out
My wife's nickname

When I awaken from my dream
My body is covered with sweat
Suzhou's spring snow is outside my window

The hand I am holding
Is in fact my own
Yet I am unable to return home

February 14, 2006 Suzhou
（Translated by Jane Deasy）

The Dairy Cow Inside the Iron Fence

The dairy cow has just given birth
The little dairy cow has just stood up
Without time to suckle its mother's milk
A stranger forcefully grabs her away

The dairy cow locked inside the iron fence
Has no space to move around
She stands the entire day gazing towards the outside
Thinking of her little baby

The little dairy cow misses her mother
And wants one mouthful of her mother's milk
And can only use her imagination

Humans don't use their mother's milk to nurture
Infants only know once they have grown up
That infant formula is made from cow's milk

Their own mother is a dairy cow
That is locked inside an iron fence

October 11, 2008
(Translated by Jane Deasy)

The White Egret

——To commemorate 228

The lonely white egret
With one leg tucked away, stands alone
Facing Ai River
Without uttering a word

The heroic departed souls that withered away long ago
Return to the scene to participate
In the commemoration events for 228
The sixty-second anniversary passes by in a flash

To think about historic wounds
Burst open once again
Fresh blood stains Yuanshan red
Sticks and batons are waiting outside the hotel

Through the entire afternoon, the white egret
Tucks one foot away and stands alone

Pondering its next step
And how to fly away

June 2009
（Translated by Jane Deasy）

The Firefly

The firefly flies a lonely flight
It comes into my study in search of his brother that has lost contact
He flies until he is very tired
And stops upon the ancient map of Taiwan

To be colonized, to be ruled by a foreign regime
Tears flow from the hand-drawn old map
To have endless exorbitant demands be made over a long period of
    time
Life has suffered persecution and threats

I nervously turn off the electric light
Fearful that an informer might make a secret report

The firefly emits light by oneself
And attempts to shine light upon the map of Taiwan

This land with historical significance
This island nation with fixed territory

June 2009
(Translated by Jane Deasy)

Reed Flower

Hurrying to attend an autumn date
The reed flower bends over to comb and groom
A head full of white hair

Bearing the pressure of the recession
The more he combs, the thinner it becomes
The more he grooms, the whiter it becomes

December 2009
(Translated by Jane Deasy)

Dewdrops

——Commemorating 30 Years of Marriage

The sunlight that just woke up
Gently touches the dewdrops
That were left on the petals last night

I focus on searching for the most beautiful viewpoint, wanting
You to become my heart's only
Dewdrop of a radiantly shining diamond

To encounter a soulmate in life
There must be principal and secondary causes, that originates from
the unknown
When the principal and secondary causes are all sufficient, only then
is it known
How hard it is

Thirty years of marriage passes by in a flash
One perceives how life is this transient

O dewdrops! You are panicking
That youth and beauty are about to disappear

I use digital images to keep
Your beautiful radiance, in my heart
It will never disappear, it will never disappear

At the same time I store the memory
In the cloud, awaiting
For old age to come and to lean on each other and accompany each
other

December 2009
(Translated by Jane Deasy)

Nonperson

My wife said

I was awakened by the sound

Of your snoring

I was alarmed to realize

That I was exhausted like a corpse

Living

My body

Has been cut into fragments by

My work

My soul

When it sees how people trample on one another

Cries

October 2010

(Translated by Jane Deasy)

The Chickens that Lead the Way

The rooster and the hen are locked together in a cage
The rooster has the action of escaping
The hen has the intention of fleeing

Locked together in an old suitcase at the same time
Married out together with the bride
From the old tribe to the big city

The carsick rooster suddenly opens his eyes
And is excited to see a thread of light
He stretches out his neck and begins to crow

Oh oh oh oh oh oh oh
The hen in the suitcase
Shuts her eyes tightly and imagines

September 2011
(Translated by Jane Deasy)

Listen to the Commands of a Master

Always when waiting for connecting flights at airports
Do I meet many wandering doves
That I am acquainted with

They come from different dovecotes
They all have different banners
Yet the all listen to the commands of a master

Following commands of their master
They toil their entire lives for their masters
Wandering all over the world

Following the purpose of their master
All one can say is: yes
And only then can one have a piece
Of a sky that does not belong to oneself

October 2011
(Translated by Jane Deasy)

Love River

Love River
We have a river in our hearts
Written full of love and romance

Love River
Love River's water slowly flows
Into the depths of time

Love River
Flows into the blood vessels to become
The inner soul's strength

Love River
Poetry and beauty
Fill up the journey of life

November 18, 2011
(Translated by Jane Deasy)

War and the Peace Memorial Park

To commemorate 228[1]
In memory of the old Taiwanese veterans
They are all suffering souls

The political executioner bloodily shoots and kills
The sound of gunfire locks the memory
Fear remains always

When authoritarian rulers step down
Can the people stop being deprived of
Their lives and property

War and the Peace Memorial Park
Those remembering have dispersed
Heroic souls linger

I see my chest

With a twenty-first century jasmine flower arranged upon it

Blooming across the whole world

Note 1:228, refers to the 228 Incident or 228 Massacre, also known as the February 28th Incident. An anti-government uprising that occurred in Taiwan. Taking its name from the date of the incident, it began on February 27, 1947.

April 15, 2013
(Translated by Jane Deasy)

Formosa Boulevard Station

He said: I want to lie down and admire
The glass artistry of the Dome of Light
In a beautiful palace of democracy and liberty
A Formosa Boulevard Station with historical significance
Let's allow the varied colors
To contain every experience of this life

Lying down, he cannot clearly see
The glass artistry of the Dome of Light
Beauty, becomes a past tense of his
He remembers standing beneath the stage on the night of the
incident
His eyes were battered by the tear gas attacks
How can an ordinary citizen withstand
The organized and planned repression by military police

Many mistakes in history

Many innocent lives sacrificed

We did not awaken the hidden bloodiness

If those stained hands behind all could promptly reflect

True democracy will not regress

People will no longer need to be opposed to each other in conflict

Visible and invisible boundaries

Disappear. Is it possible?

He said: People! They only lie down when dead

Admiring the glass artistry of the Dome of Light

In a beautiful palace of democracy and liberty

A Formosa Boulevard Station with historical significance

June 2013

(Translated by Jane Deasy)

Coffee of the Heart

My hands hold the same coffee cup
But my heart has a different shape

Tasting the same Dongshan single origin coffee
My heart interprets each color, aroma, taste

Life's journey of happiness, joy, anger, sorrow
Explained through language, words, musical notes, paint

The world of coffee is full of imagination
No borders, no boundaries, free to roam

Ah! The formless aroma of coffee
Lets the soul abundantly free

August 30, 2013
(Translated by Jane Deasy)

Maple Red

Maple red is the face of the season
Imbued with poeticism and hidden sadness

The kind of beauty that most makes souls pulsate
Carrying my camera I pursue onto Aowanda
Twice in two years all I see is a ground full of fallen leaves

I want to pick some for souvenirs
My emotions fall into the maple red's depths
My feet are unable to move

September 2013
(Translated by Jane Deasy)

Journey Through Taiwanese Tea Mountains

A journey through Taiwanese tea mountains
Tea is in the heart
People are in the painting

Pay a visit to the tea-making expert
Taste the fragrance of the tea, know the sun and the moon
The essence, all in a cup of tea

My nose is greeted by the fragrance of tea
An abundant aroma of tea
Smoothly guiding the internal organs
Easing the twelve meridians

Taiwanese tea is a sweet spring
Warming Taiwanese hearts
Enriching Taiwanese lives

October 2013
(Translated by Jane Deasy)

People

People live and die by fate
People come and go by reincarnation

A person's soul leaves a body
A person's soul attaches to a body

People leave families of this world
People come to families of this world

After busily rushing about
People return to the homes where they were born
Calm the heart to study
The Perfection of Transcendent Wisdom

Two hundred and sixty words contain vast truths
Each word is a light-emitting
Planet in the heavens

Listen quietly to droplets quickly falling off the eaves of the ancestral
home
It must be the dew imposing a cool and refreshing sound
Home, echoes through this life

February 2014
（Translated by Jane Deasy）

A Poet Makes Pottery

I use hands that have written many poems
To freely mold many teacups
Not seeking smoothness, not seeking perfection
Each has a form, round-like but not round
Corresponding to real life
Where once molded, a touch must remain

I use hands that have written many poems
To shape clay on a potter's wheel
Shaping life into a circle
The malleability of the clay
Inspires my creativity to continue
Exploring forms of artistic expression

February 2014
(Translated by Jane Deasy)

The Internet

The internet, has everything
Fingers slide here and there
To hypnotize yourself
That there are no distances on the internet

Click a 'like'
Add a friend, a fan page
LINE to, LINE fro
Always keeping on standby

More and more people's egos
Are controlled by smartphones
Like developing a drug addiction
With recurrent seizures

In internet communities
Every person is searching for
A lonely existence

June 15, 2014
(Translated by Jane Deasy)

Boundaries

My thoughts

Follow the wind

And pass through

Human-defined sea territory

Human-defined national boundaries

Human-defined time

Human-defined space

Boundaries

All do not exist

Entirely　vanish

September 15, 2014]

（Translated by Jane Deasy）

Man and the Sea

Mankind, generation after generation
With a greedy heart
Wants to possess the sea

The sea, each hour and each minute
Washes with its waves
Mankind's greedy heart

September 15, 2014
(Translated by Jane Deasy)

Starlight

The sky is filled with starlight
There is no pollution here
Someone faces the starry sky
For a long exposure

And leaves a trail of the stars
A beautiful trail of light
If a circle is formed
I would even smile in my dreams

Immeasurable planets
Endlessly in motion
Asking who will converge with the vast universe

So much inconceivable, unfathomable

Life, on distant planets

Waving, calling out to people on earth

April 27, 2014
（Translated by Jane Deasy）

Lights of the Fireflies

The national forestlands are without pollution
In the dark of the night, fireflies swarm and fly
Lights speckle, measuring coldy

Living in a pressure cooker
The modern man, has a need to come here
To receive the benediction of the fireflies

Flickering with a faint luminescence
Heals the depths of modern man's soul
A nameless sort of emptiness

Someone, faces the lights of the fireflies
For a long exposure
And leaves a beautiful trail of light

A mysterious abstract painting
A cursive script left when
The angels were a little drunk

April 27, 2014
(Translated by Jane Deasy)

The Alangyi Ancient Trail Map

Chinook winds whistle among the trees
Wind and rain cannot stop us
Relying on a rich imagination and expectation
A trip is made along the Alangyi Ancient Trail

Giant waves pound over and over against the coast
Strong wind from the ocean bitterly hits my face
One can only walk sideways against the wind and bow one's head
And follow the footsteps of our forefathers to advance ahead

By one's ear the of beat of a drum sounds out
It is far-gone history's echo
Until today it remains here
Beating between the cliff and the coast

One day scrolls and moves hundreds of years of history
To find oneself in such a vast scene

Moved from the depths of life
Each person has seared a long scroll of
The Alangyi Ancient Trail Map

October 20, 2015
（Translated by Jane Deasy）

About the Author

Lee Chang-hsien was born in Tainan and is currently living in Kaohsiung City. He has previously participated in Forest Poetry Society, Green Poetry Society, Little Sunshine Collection, and Li Poetry Society. He has worked as a manager at a listed electronics company. His creative works mainly lie in poetry, seal carving, pottery, and photography. He is currently the editor-in-chief of Li Poetry Journal and a seal carving teacher at the Kaohsiung First Community University.

In June 1981, he published his first collection of poetry, *Poems of the Processing Zone*, and in 1982 he won the Li Poetry Award. Other poetry collections published include *Ecology Collection* (1993), *On the Production Line* (1996), *Looking Up at the Starry Skies* (2005), *From Youth to Grey Hair* (2005), *Portraits of Taiwanese Poets-The Chang-hsien Li Poetry Anthology* (2007), *Selected Works of a Taiwanese Poet- The Chang-hsien Li Collection* (2010), *A*

Vision of Beauty- Slow Travel in Greater Kaohsiung Poetry and Photography Collection (2014), *Poetics of Kaohsiung 1977-2015* (2016). Lines from his poem *Song of Expectation* was selected into the Kaohsiung City Literature Trail; his poems *Overtime* and *Ruthless Enterprises* were selected in *Selected Works of Chinese Literature for Universities of Technology*; his work is published in annual poetry selections, national and international poetry collections, and has been translated and introduced in English, Japanese, Korean, and Mongolian.

About the Translators

William Marr has published 23 volumes of poetry (two in English and the rest in his native Chinese language), 3 books of essays, and several books of translations. His poetry has been translated into more than ten languages and included in over one hundred anthologies. Some of his poems are used in high school and college textbooks in Taiwan, China, England, and Germany. He is a former president of the Illinois State Poetry Society and has received numerous honors, including several awards from Taiwan, China, and U.S.A. for his poetry and translations. He now lives in the Chicago area.

Wen-hsiung Hsu, is Professor Emeritus at Northwestern University where he taught for 35 years from 1969 to 2004. In 2007-2011 he was Distinguished Professor of History at his alma mater Tunghai University. A Tunghai graduate in 1962, he also received his M. A. from Harvard, Ph.D. from the University of Chicago, and did postdoctoral study in English social history at Oxford's Balliol Collage.

Jane Deasy is an Irish-born, Taiwan-raised, Vancouver-based Mandarin Chinese Translator and Interpreter.

She is an Associate Member of The Society of Translators and Interpreters of British Columbia and a Member of the Literary Translators' Association of Canada (Concordia University, Montreal).

CONTENTS

語言文學類　PG1980　台灣詩叢05

愛河 Love River
——李昌憲漢英雙語詩集

作　　者／李昌憲（Lee Chang-hsien）
譯　　者／非馬（William Marr）、許達然（Wen-hsiung Hsu）、
　　　　　戴珍妮（Jane Deasy）
叢書策劃／李魁賢（Lee Kuei-shien）
責任編輯／林昕平
圖文排版／周妤靜
封面設計／蔡瑋筠

發 行 人／宋政坤
法律顧問／毛國樑　律師
出版發行／秀威資訊科技股份有限公司
　　　　　114台北市內湖區瑞光路76巷65號1樓
　　　　　電話：+886-2-2796-3638　傳真：+886-2-2796-1377
　　　　　http://www.showwe.com.tw
劃撥帳號／19563868　戶名：秀威資訊科技股份有限公司
　　　　　讀者服務信箱：service@showwe.com.tw
展售門市／國家書店（松江門市）
　　　　　104台北市中山區松江路209號1樓
　　　　　電話：+886-2-2518-0207　傳真：+886-2-2518-0778
網路訂購／秀威網路書店：https://store.showwe.tw
　　　　　國家網路書店：https://www.govbooks.com.tw

2018年3月　BOD一版
定價：260元

國家圖書館出版品預行編目

愛河 Love River : 李昌憲漢英雙語詩集 / 李昌憲著 ; 非馬 , 許達然 , 戴珍妮譯. -- 一版. -- 臺北市 : 秀威資訊科技, 2018.03
面 ; 公分. -- (台灣詩叢 ; 5)
BOD版
ISBN 978-986-326-525-2(平裝)

851.486 107000452

讀者回函卡

感謝您購買本書，為提升服務品質，請填妥以下資料，將讀者回函卡直接寄回或傳真本公司，收到您的寶貴意見後，我們會收藏記錄及檢討，謝謝！如您需要了解本公司最新出版書目、購書優惠或企劃活動，歡迎您上網查詢或下載相關資料：http:// www.showwe.com.tw

您購買的書名：＿＿＿＿＿＿＿＿＿＿＿＿＿＿＿＿＿＿＿＿

出生日期：＿＿＿＿年＿＿＿＿月＿＿＿＿日

學歷：□高中（含）以下　□大專　□研究所（含）以上

職業：□製造業　□金融業　□資訊業　□軍警　□傳播業　□自由業
　　　□服務業　□公務員　□教職　□學生　□家管　□其它＿＿＿

購書地點：□網路書店　□實體書店　□書展　□郵購　□贈閱　□其他

您從何得知本書的消息？

□網路書店　□實體書店　□網路搜尋　□電子報　□書訊　□雜誌
□傳播媒體　□親友推薦　□網站推薦　□部落格　□其他＿＿＿＿＿

您對本書的評價：（請填代號　1.非常滿意　2.滿意　3.尚可　4.再改進）

封面設計＿＿　版面編排＿＿　內容＿＿　文／譯筆＿＿　價格＿＿

讀完書後您覺得：

□很有收穫　□有收穫　□收穫不多　□沒收穫

對我們的建議：＿＿＿＿＿＿＿＿＿＿＿＿＿＿＿＿＿＿＿＿

＿＿＿＿＿＿＿＿＿＿＿＿＿＿＿＿＿＿＿＿＿＿＿＿＿＿

＿＿＿＿＿＿＿＿＿＿＿＿＿＿＿＿＿＿＿＿＿＿＿＿＿＿

＿＿＿＿＿＿＿＿＿＿＿＿＿＿＿＿＿＿＿＿＿＿＿＿＿＿

請貼
郵票

11466
台北市內湖區瑞光路 76 巷 65 號 1 樓
秀威資訊科技股份有限公司 收
BOD 數位出版事業部

（請沿線對折寄回，謝謝！）

姓　　名：＿＿＿＿＿＿＿＿　年齡：＿＿＿＿　性別：□女　□男

郵遞區號：□□□□□

地　　址：＿＿＿＿＿＿＿＿＿＿＿＿＿＿＿＿

聯絡電話：（日）＿＿＿＿＿＿＿＿（夜）＿＿＿＿＿＿＿＿

E-mail：＿＿＿＿＿＿＿＿＿＿＿＿＿＿＿＿